DEC 11 '89	DATE DUE		
APR 9	SEP 11 97	JAN 03 '92	
JUL 2 90	AUG 19 '99		
SEP 2 0	MAY 1 6 2000		
APR 17	APR 2 1 2001		
MAY 4	APR 4 - 2002		
	MAY 2 9 2002		
APR 8 '92	AUG 2 5 2001		
DEC 92			
APR 2 2 8	JUN 4 8		
9			

SUBJECT TO LATE FINE

About the Book

Porcupine Baby was not afraid. The quills on his back were hard and sharp. He had learned quickly how to protect himself with them.

So when Porcupine Baby went out by himself one night, he was feeling very brave. But he soon learned that a wise fox can outsmart a careless porcupine!

Berniece Freschet and Jim Arnosky join their skills of observation and knowledge of nature to create the early experiences of a baby animal for the very young.

PORCUPINE BABY

by Berniece Freschet

A SEE AND READ NATURE STORY

with pictures by Jim Arnosky

G.P. Putnam's Sons   New York

For Liam and Brendan

Text copyright © 1978 by Berniece Freschet
Illustrations copyright © 1978 by Jim Arnosky
All rights reserved. Published simultaneously
in Canada by Longman Canada Limited, Toronto.
Printed in the United States of America
06209
Library of Congress Cataloging in Publication Data
Freschet, Berniece. Porcupine Baby.
1. Porcupines—Juvenile literature. 2. Animals,
Infancy of—Juvenile literature. [1. Porcupines]
I. Arnosky, Jim. II. Title
QL737.R652F73   599'3234   77-4199
ISBN 0-399-61101-0 lib. bdg.

Contents

THE BOLD ONE

The newborn porcupine
was one hour old.
He was bigger
than most newborn babies.
Porcupine Baby was almost
as big as a full-grown squirrel.

In their den,

a hollow place

between some rocks,

Mother Porcupine sat up

on her haunches and tail.

Porcupine Baby began to nurse

his mother's good milk.

The newborn porcupine
had no brothers
and no sisters.
He was the only baby.
Sometimes a mother porcupine
gives birth to two babies,
but never more than two.

Even though Porcupine Baby

was only one hour old

he was covered with dark brown fur.

His eyes were open.

The sharp quills on his back

had already hardened.

He even had some teeth.

When his stomach was full
of the warm milk,
the little porcupine gave
a small grunt and went to sleep.

In a few days Porcupine Baby
began to nibble on tender leaves.
He was a very bold and curious
little porcupine.
He pushed his nose
under every log
and into every bush.

When he was two weeks old
he was big enough to get
along on his own.

And he was not afraid.

But still, he stayed
with his mother
for a while longer.
Each day when the sun
went down behind the hill,
Porcupine Baby and his mother
began their hunt for food.
They waddled slowly
through the woods,
eating leaves and twigs.

They stopped beside
a wild gooseberry bush
to eat the sweet berries.

Then they ambled on down
the path to the stream
to dig up juicy roots
and nibble on the stems
of pond lilies.

In winter,

when food is hard to find,

sometimes a porcupine

will eat the bark from trees.

If they pull off

too much bark,

the tree will die.

If the trees happen to be
in the farmer's apple orchard,
the farmer calls his dog
and they go hunting for porcupine.

All night long,
under a bright moon,
Porcupine Baby and his mother
hunted for food.
But when the moon went down
and the first rays of the sun
began to slide over the hills,
the porcupines looked
for a place to rest.
Porcupine Baby was tired
from the long night's hunt.
The bold little porcupine
climbed a tall pine tree.

He stretched out on a limb.

His four feet dangled

down on each side.

He gave a small grunt

and slept there

for the rest of the day.

And he was not afraid.

A SECRET WEAPON

Porcupine Baby loved
the taste of salt.
Once he found
a set of antlers,
shed by a deer.
He began to chew them.
He liked the salty taste
in the antlers.

Early one morning
Porcupine Baby and his mother
were walking by the stream,
looking for a place to rest,
when they came to a canoe.

The porcupines began to chew
on the paddle handles,
tasting the salt left there
from the sweat of hands.

Close by,

a red fox watched

from the bushes.

Suddenly,

the fox jumped out—

right in front of the porcupines.

But the fox did not scare

the mother porcupine.

She had met foxes before.

Quickly, she turned
her back to the enemy.
She bristled her quills.

All over her body,
from the top of her head
to the tip of her tail,
sharp, spiny quills stood up.
His instincts told Porcupine Baby
to do the same.

The porcupines looked like
two round pin cushions
—one big,
and one little.

Most animals learn to keep
a safe distance from porcupines.

But the fox was young,
and had not yet learned
this lesson.
He moved closer.

SLAP!

Mother Porcupine's tail

hit him on the paw.

The fox leaped back

yelping with pain.

He limped away and sat down.

With his teeth he pulled

the sharp quills from his paw.

Porcupine Baby was not big.

He could not run fast.

He did not have sharp teeth

to defend himself.

He was not a fighter.

But Porcupine Baby was *not afraid*,

because he had

his own special weapon,

an armor of quills.

If Porcupine Baby met an enemy,
he could stiffen his quills
until they stood high—

just like the hair
on a frightened cat.

If the enemy was foolish and
came too close,

Porcupine Baby would lash out
with his tail.

The loose quills in his skin came
out easily.

They would stick his enemy
on the nose or paws.
Now Porcupine Baby knew
why he had few enemies
to fear.

Brave and bold,
he waddled down the path.

THE SMART FOX

One bright, moonlit night,
Porcupine Baby was on his
way to the stream.
He was four weeks old now
and on his own.

At the stream,

he sat by the water

and nibbled a juicy stem

from a pond lily.

Other night hunters were out

looking for their suppers.

Across the stream,

a shy possum dug in the sand,

looking for turtle eggs to eat.

He heard the hunting cry
of the barn owl. "Whoo…whooo!"
Close by, a raccoon dipped
a plump persimmon into the water.

In the woods,
a fox moved quietly
through the trees.
He was hungry, too.
He came to the path
that led to the stream.

Porcupine Baby climbed
up the bank to eat leaves
from a wild geranium bush.

The hungry fox soon
came to the stream.
He sniffed the air.
He saw Porcupine Baby.
He slunk low to the ground.

The fox crept close…
closer!

Now he was close enough.

He jumped out at the porcupine!

Quickly, Porcupine Baby

turned his back.

He bristled his quills.

He rolled himself into a tight ball.

But he was not really afraid.

37

He had met a fox before,
and the fox had limped away.
But this was not that young,
inexperienced fox.
This was an older, wiser fox
who knew that if he could

flip the baby porcupine

on his back,

he would be helpless.

There were no quills to protect

a porcupine on his undersides.

The fox waited.

For just a second,

Porcupine Baby was careless —

      he lifted his head.

Quick as a flash

the fox's paw shot out!

He caught the porcupine
under his chin
and flipped him high.
Porcupine Baby somersaulted
into the air!

Down he came,
right on the edge of the bank,
a round ball of quills.

The fox jumped after him.

His paw slapped out.

Down the bank rolled Porcupine Baby

—head over heels

—end over end.

This time Porcupine Baby was afraid.

SPLASH!

He rolled right into the stream.

Porcupine Baby's hollow quills
helped him to float.
His head bobbed out of the water.

He paddled his feet.
Like most animals
Porcupine Baby was a good swimmer.
The water carried him downstream.

Porcupine Baby climbed

up on the opposite bank.

What a sight he was!

—leaves and twigs stuck out

all over his coat.

He shook himself and grunted.

He had been lucky.

He had escaped the fox.

But his lack of fear

had made him careless.

And he had almost been caught.

Tonight he learned

an important lesson.

Porcupine Baby pushed

up the bank and slowly

made his way back to the woods.

A cold, north wind blew
down from the hills,
rustling through the grasses,
and ruffling the fur
on the porcupine's back.
The long, cold winter
would soon be here.
But Porcupine Baby's thick coat
of fur would keep him warm
even when snows were deep.

Porcupine Baby crawled

into a hollow stump.

He rolled up into

a tight ball of fur.

He gave a small grunt.

He was not afraid.

About the Author

Berniece Freschet was educated in her native Montana, first in Miles City and then in Missoula, where she attended the University of Montana.

She now lives in Rockville Centre, New York, with her husband and five children.

In 1974 Mrs. Freschet won both the Irma Simonton Black Award and the New York Academy of Sciences Children's Book Award.

About the Artist

Jim Arnosky is a self-taught artist who lives with his wife and two daughters in Ryegate, Vermont.

Jim's activities vary with the seasons. He fishes, hikes, gardens, and bird- and animal-watches, and, of course, draws all year round.

He is the author/illustrator of the Putnam book I WAS BORN IN A TREE AND RAISED BY BEES.